THE STORY OF MISS MOPPET

THE STORY OF
MISS MOPPET

BY

BEATRIX POTTER

Author of
"The Tale of Peter Rabbit," &c.

FREDERICK WARNE

The reproductions in this book have been made using the most modern electronic scanning methods from entirely new transparencies of Beatrix Potter's original watercolours. They enable Beatrix Potter's skill as an artist to be appreciated as never before, not even during her own lifetime.

FREDERICK WARNE

Penguin Books Ltd, 27 Wrights Lane, London W8 5TZ (Publishing and Editorial)
and Harmondsworth, Middlesex, England (Distribution and Warehouse)
Viking Penguin Inc., 40 West 23rd Street, New York, New York 10010, U.S.A.
Penguin Books Australia Ltd, Ringwood, Victoria, Australia
Penguin Books Canada Limited, 2801 John Street, Markham, Ontario, Canada L3R 1B4
Penguin Books (N.Z.) Ltd, 182–190 Wairau Road, Auckland 10, New Zealand

First published 1906
This edition with new reproductions first published 1987
This impression 1987

Colour reproduction by
East Anglian Engraving Company Ltd, Norwich
Printed and bound in Great Britain by
William Clowes Limited, Beccles and London

1187

THIS is a Pussy called Miss Moppet, she thinks she has heard a mouse !

THIS is the Mouse peeping out behind the cupboard, and making fun of Miss Moppet. He is not afraid of a kitten.

THIS is Miss Moppet jumping just too late; she misses the Mouse and hits her own head.

SHE thinks it is a very hard cupboard!

THE Mouse watches Miss Moppet from the top of the cupboard.

MISS MOPPET ties up her head in a duster, and sits before the fire.

THE Mouse thinks she is looking very ill. He comes sliding down the bell-pull.

MISS MOPPET looks worse and worse. The Mouse comes a little nearer.

MISS MOPPET holds her poor head in her paws, and looks at him through a hole in the duster. The Mouse comes *very* close.

AND then all of a sudden —Miss Moppet jumps upon the Mouse!

AND because the Mouse has teased Miss Moppet — Miss Moppet thinks she will tease the Mouse; which is not at all nice of Miss Moppet.

SHE ties him up in the duster, and tosses it about like a ball.

BUT she forgot about that hole in the duster ; and when she untied it — there was no Mouse !

HE has wriggled out and run away; and he is dancing a jig on the top of the cupboard!

The "PETER RABBIT" BOOKS
by BEATRIX POTTER
PETER RABBIT · SQUIRREL NUTKIN
TAILOR OF GLOUCESTER · BENJAMIN BUNNY
TWO BAD MICE · MRS. TIGGY-WINKLE
MR. JEREMY FISHER · TOM KITTEN
JEMIMA PUDDLE-DUCK · THE FLOPSY BUNNIES
MRS. TITTLEMOUSE · TIMMY TIPTOES
JOHNNY TOWN-MOUSE · MR. TOD
PIGLING BLAND · SAMUEL WHISKERS
THE PIE & THE PATTY-PAN · GINGER & PICKLES
LITTLE PIG ROBINSON
A FIERCE BAD RABBIT
APPLEY DAPPLY'S NURSERY RHYMES
PETER RABBIT'S PAINTING BOOK
MISS MOPPET
CECILY PARSLEY'S NURSERY RHYMES
TOM KITTEN'S PAINTING BOOK